Russ and the Almost Perfect Day

Janet Elizabeth Rickert

Photographs by Pete McGahan

WOODBINE HOUSE ■ 2000

Dedicated to:

Sandra Tuzik
William LeMonnier
Jackie Phelan

Library of Congress Cataloging-in-Publication Data

Rickert, Janet Elizabeth.
    Russ and the almost perfect day / by Janet Elizabeth Rickert ; photographs by Pete McGahan—1st ed.
        p. cm.
    Summary: Russ, a student with Down syndrome, is having a perfect day until he realizes that the five-dollar bill he has found probably belongs to a classmate.
    ISBN 1-890627-18-6 (hardcover)
    [1. Lost and found possessions—Fiction. 2. Schools—Fiction. 3. Down syndrome—Fiction. 4. Mentally handicapped—Fiction.]
I. McGahan, Pete, ill, II. Title.

PZ7.R41612 Rs 2000
[E]—dc21   00-063336

Manufactured in Hong Kong

First edition

10 9 8 7 6 5 4 3 2 1

Second, Russ's favorite TV show was still on, even after he had brushed his teeth, washed his face, buttoned his shirt, packed his backpack, and fed his fish!

And then, while walking to school with Kevin, Russ found a 5 dollar bill.

Good things kept happening even after Russ got to school. First, Russ got to help raise the flag.

Then, David invited him to his birthday party as soon as Russ walked into the classroom.

In math class, the teacher showed a video. Unbelievable!

In gym, the teacher let everyone ride scooters...

...and then play with hula hoops outside!

In science class, Russ got to see a special exhibit of cold-blooded creatures. Hearing about cold-blooded creatures suddenly reminded Russ of the ice cream he was going to buy at lunch.

When Russ went to the library, he was thrilled to find the fire truck book he had been waiting for since last month.

Russ's day was going so great, he didn't even mind taking the social studies test.

Russ grabbed a vanilla ice cream cone with chocolate fudge sauce—his favorite. While Kevin was deciding between an ice cream sandwich and an ice cream cone, Russ noticed a girl crying. "It was right in my pocket," she said to the lunchroom aide. "It must have fallen out on my way to school."

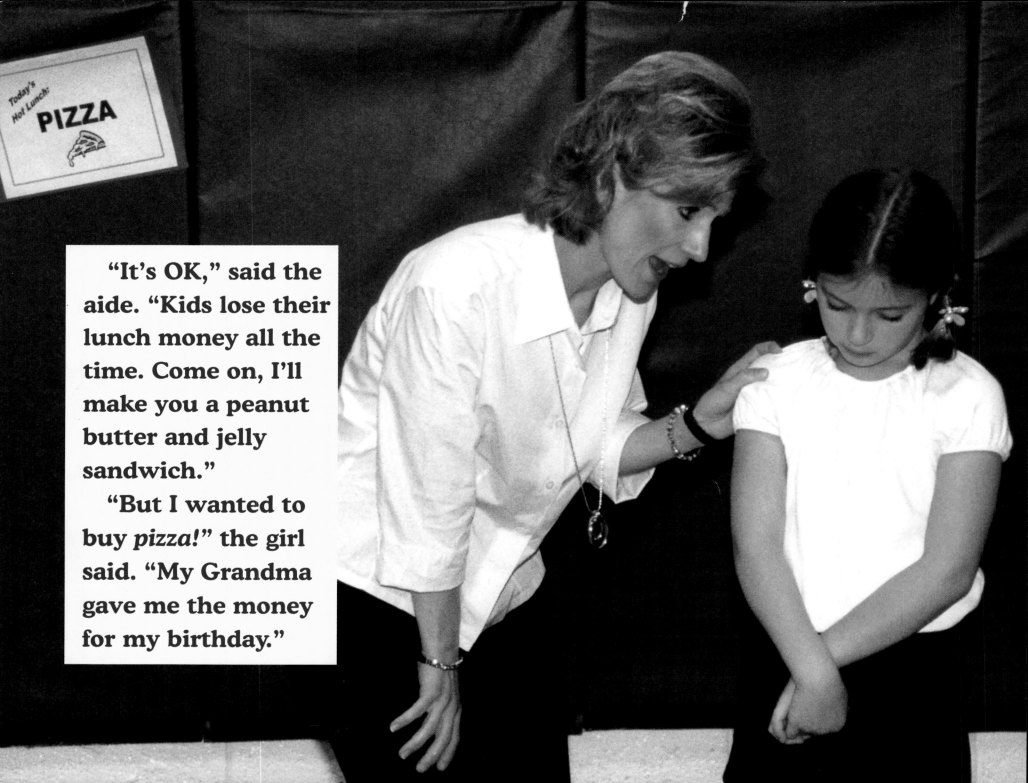

"It's OK," said the aide. "Kids lose their lunch money all the time. Come on, I'll make you a peanut butter and jelly sandwich."

"But I wanted to buy *pizza!*" the girl said. "My Grandma gave me the money for my birthday."

Today's Hot Lunch: PIZZA

"Uh oh," said Kevin. "Are you thinking what I'm thinking?"

"Yeah," said Russ. He looked down at the ice cream cone in his hand. His mouth watered as he imagined taking a big bite of vanilla ice cream and crackly sweet fudge. Then he slowly pulled the $5 bill out of his pocket. "What should I do?" he asked Kevin.

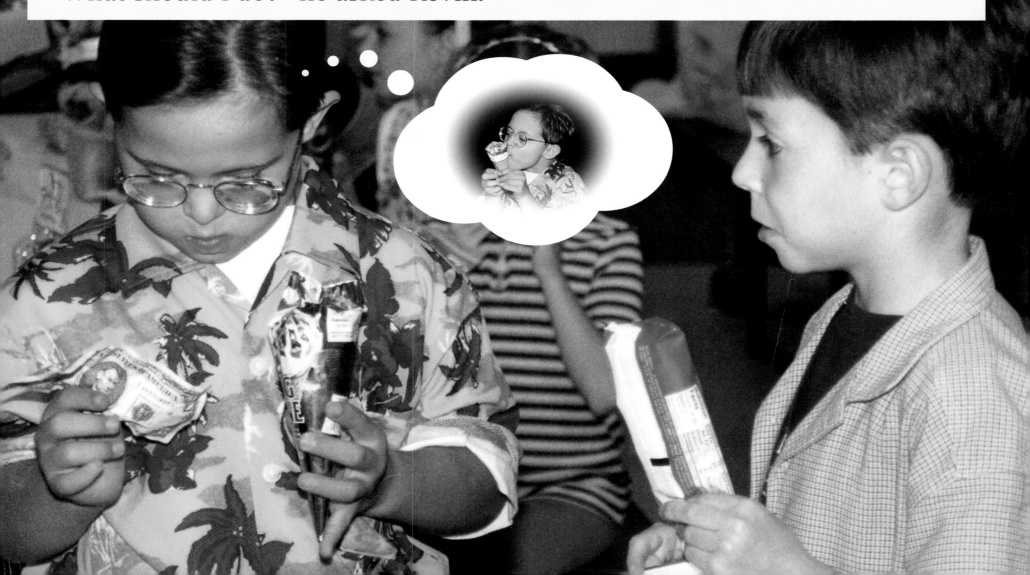

"We don't *know* it's her money," said Kevin. "It could be anyone's."

"Next, please," said the woman at the cash register. "You boys want that ice cream or not?"

"Yes," said Russ, "I *do* want it." He looked at the crying girl again. And then ever so slowly, he put the ice cream cone back in the cooler.

Russ and Kevin walked over to the girl. "Is this your lunch money?"

"Yes!" the girl said, sniffling. "Thank you so much!" She wiped her eyes on her sleeve and beamed at Russ.

"You're welcome," said Russ, smiling back. He wasn't sure why, but he felt happy inside.

The aide patted him on the back. "Russ, that was very honest of you," she said. "I'm proud of you."

"Yeah," said Kevin. "Maybe losers weepers isn't such a good idea."

I'm so proud of you, Russ.

Russ and Kevin hurried to join the other kids on the playground. Luckily, they were still in time to get a basketball.

That recess, Russ made three baskets! And the net wasn't even lowered.

And when Russ got back to class he got to see the new class pet, a turtle!

As Russ and Kevin were leaving school, it started pouring down rain . . . but that's another story!

Special Thanks to:

Ridge School

Mr. LeMonnier, Principal
Mrs. Prato, Assistant Principal
Carol Anderson
Cathy Borden
Donna Christakos
Linda Evans
Diane Jennings
Laurel Kasang
Lynn Kuzmenka
Carey Murphy
Jackie Phelan
Carol Super
Nancy Trandel
Shari Vrba

Students

Melanie Beth
Adam Bird
Brittany Bird
Corey Boudreau
Patrice Burke
Sean Conlon
Tom Conlon
Justin DeChristopher
Daniel Decker
Thomas Deery
Lyndsay Doyle
Josh Gazdziak
Tia Gazdziak
Lauren Hall
Katie Herman
Lyndsey Herman
Marissa Herman

Laura Kabak
Sean Klimson
Alex Koranda
Marissa Koranda
Mathew Lowczyk
Lucas Madel
Christina McLaughlin
Nicole Minik
Cassie Nativo
Kirk Peterson
Cheyenne Ramos
Alex Regets
Justin Rickert
Mike Rickert
Sirena Rodriguez
Kayla Roeske

Tyler Roeske
Mike Schipits
Shannon Seibt
Timothy Seibt
David Sheehan
Rachel Sinon
Jennifer Spreadbury
Andrew Suddreth
Taylor Suddreth
Brook Telander
Scott Telander
Kevin Walsh
Craig Williams

Others

Brittany Burke
Blondie *(the snake)*
Bonnie *(the bunny)*
Kyle Considine
Brian Donoghue
Lauren Fishback
Chris Gazdziak
Jean Hunt
Donna Knieps
Yvonne Mattz
Beverly Minik *(plays the part of Mom)*
Morgan Minik
Vanessa Minik
Mark Rickert
Scott Rickert
Bob Telander
Therese Telander
Sandra Nowak (Tuzik)

Art Lynn Photography
Brock Leach, President, Frito-Lay, Inc.
Jewel Food Stores, Oak Forest, Illinois
Jim Nesci, Cold Blooded Creatures, Inc.
Sodexho—Marriott
Stuart Sorkin, President, Affy Tapple, Inc.
Working Class Uniforms